Kestrels 3

Cross-country Gallop

Other Patricia Leitch stories you will enjoy

The Kestrels series

The Jinny series

Kestrels 3

Cross-country Gallop

Patricia Leitch

Illustrated by Elsie Lennox

Lions
An Imprint of HarperCollinsPublishers

First published in Great Britain in Lions in 1993
1 3 5 7 9 10 8 6 4 2

Lions is an imprint of HarperCollins Children's Books,
a division of HarperCollins Publishers Ltd, 77–85 Fulham
Palace Road, Hammersmith, London W6 8JB

Text copyright © Patricia Leitch 1993
Illustrations copyright © Elsie Lennox 1993
ISBN 0 00 694087 0

The author asserts the moral right to be identified as the
author of the work

Printed and bound in Great Britain
by HarperCollins Book Manufacturing Ltd, Glasgow

Chapter One

Sally Lorimer was nine years old. She was not tall, not small; not fat not skinny. Her thick brown hair grew straight to her shoulders and was cut into a fringe. She had wide-set blue eyes and a quirky mouth that turned up at the corners. Sprawled out on the long grass that grew like a meadow round the ruined summerhouse she stared out at the glint and glimmer of the summer sea. Behind her was the overgrown garden that reached to the high, stone tower of Kestrels – a huge stone house, built on its own peninsula of land, where Sally and her family lived.

Stretched out at Sally's side lay Thalia ("Rhymes-with-dahlia-which-is-a-flower-like-a-chrysanthemum") Nisbet. Thalia, too, was nine years old. She was long and lean with a fizzing sunburst of corn-coloured hair. Thalia's parents were divorced and she lived with her narg – gran spelt backwards – in a cottage by the shore close to Kestrels.

"She did mean it, didn't she?" Sally demanded, turning her head so that she could see the ponies' field with its wide-spreading chestnut tree and its new fencing. She had to sit up to see the ponies – Tarquin, the sleek, almost thoroughbred roan pony who belonged to Thalia, and grazing close beside him was Willow, her own dapple-grey with a silver mane and tail.

"Yes, she meant it," said Thalia propping herself up on one elbow and grinning with delight at sea, sun and grazing ponies. "Martine said she was very pleased with our progress; that we had both improved beyond belief. Though you could hardly hear her for that man shouting at the boy. But that is what she said."

" 'Improved beyond belief'," said Sally repeating the words like a charm. Magic words, as magic as the tiny crystal unicorn she had found when she had been standing at the edge of the sea and had crouched down to discover what it was that was glinting under the water. A wave had carried it into the palm of her hand as if the sea had given it to her.

Sally searched in the pocket of her jodhs and set the unicorn in the centre of her hand. Rainbow light sparkled from it.

Did it all happen because of the unicorn? wondered Sally. Because it found me? Was waiting for me?

She shut her eyes and tried to remember back to the beginning, six long months ago, when the Lorimers had gone for a picnic at Fintry bay.

There were six human Lorimers – Mr Lorimer who was a librarian; Mrs Lorimer who painted landscapes in flowing watercolours and was only busy-about-the-house when there was absolutely nothing else worth doing. Ben

Lorimer was fifteen and the oldest child. He was tall with a shock of black hair like his father's and always had his nose in a book. Emma Lorimer was twelve with long fair hair. She could sing and dance as easily as she breathed. Sally fitted in next and then Jamie, the youngest Lorimer, who was four.

The day of the picnic was the day Sally had found the unicorn; the day they drove past Kestrels, empty and deserted and Mr Lorimer stopped the car at the foot of Kestrels' drive to let them dream for a minute about what it would be like if only they had enough money to buy the house and come and live there.

Then, thought Sally, we were an ordinary family living in a dull, ordinary house, suffocated by car fumes and noise. And me just dying because I didn't have a pony of my own, dragging up and down the lane at Miss Meek's riding school. But then everything changed.

The very next Friday *the* letter had arrived for Mr Lorimer. A great-uncle whom Mr Lorimer had hardly known had died in Australia. He had left what the solicitors called 'a considerable sum of money' to Mr Lorimer and in an almost unimaginable, magical happening they had bought Kestrels and now were all living there. Thalia was Sally's friend and kept Tarquin with Willow.

"Willow, my own pony . . ." and Sally opened her eyes to gaze lovingly at the dapple-grey pony whisking flies away with sweeps of her long, silver tail.

Until Sally had found Willow her riding had been in a bit of a mess. There had been her disastrous runaway ride on Tarquin, leaving Sally afraid to gallop. Then she had found Willow and everything had changed, until now, after a course of jumping lessons, Sally's jumping had improved so much that Martine Dawes, their instructress at Mr Frazer's posh riding school, had said, and Sally repeated the words yet again, " 'Improved beyond belief'."

"Do you think she said that because she saw us jumping the wall with Nick Ross?" she asked Thalia.

"Thirty foot spread," exaggerated Thalia. "At least twenty feet high."

Yesterday when they had been riding in a pageant Sally and Thalia had jumped into a walled garden, riding behind Nick Ross on his famous show-jumper, Rose of Sharon.

"Forty feet?" suggested Sally, and she rolled out on the warm grass, reliving the moment when Willow had soared over the wall and she had sat, securely balanced, loving every minute of it.

"Perfect!" said Thalia. "Absolutely perfect. And now Tarent Show on Saturday. Showjumping and pairs cross-country."

At Thalia's words Sally felt her stomach tighten nervously. Saturday would be the first time she had jumped in a competition. Suppose she fell off? Suppose she made a fool of Willow? Perhaps she should have stayed at Miss Meek's riding school; perhaps all she was fit for was to ride Miss Meek's shabby ponies up and down the lane.

Do not be so stupid, Sally told herself. You have left all that behind you.

But she hadn't. There was still something; something she had pushed to the back of her mind; something she couldn't allow herself to think about.

Suddenly Willow buckled at the knees and rolled over to rub and scratch herself into the ground. Three times she pushed herself off from side to side, her shoes flashing white fire, before she struggled upright, stretched out her neck, and, balancing herself on propped legs, shook herself violently.

And in the instant Sally knew. Couldn't stop herself remembering. For that was the way Miss Meek's ponies had rolled after their hard day's work in the riding school. Sally had loved all the ponies in the riding school but especially a black pony called Clover. She had been the pony that Sally had always ridden; the pony that might have been grazing in the field with Tarquin if Sally hadn't told her father that she did not want Clover, did not want him to buy a riding-school pony for her. In her mind's eye Sally saw Clover standing in her wired strip of field,

11

trying to nibble at the overgrazed grass, the saddle mark still frosted on her back.

And I turned and left her, Sally thought, and because the memory hurt so much she had to talk to Thalia about it.

"Remember I told you about Miss Meek's riding school? In Matwood where I used to ride. Remember Clover? How I told Dad I didn't want her?"

"Well, you didn't," stated Thalia. "She didn't sound to me as if she would have been much use."

"But maybe now I've improved a bit, perhaps . . ."

"You wouldn't have improved if you hadn't been riding Willow. If you had let your dad buy Clover you'd never have found Willow. True?"

"Suppose so . . ."

"TRUE," said Thalia. "So don't start. Now, where are we going to practise for the cross-country? Haven't much time to build a course but we could build some jumps in the field so we can practise jumping together. Really we only have four days because I've to go to the dentist on Wednesday."

"Right," agreed Sally, realising suddenly that it was only five days until Tarent Show.

"The obstacles won't be very big. What the judges want to see is us keeping together between the jumps and taking off and landing at exactly the same time. Whee!" and Thalia's arm traced a wide arc against sea and sky making Sally wonder just what size the obstacles would really be. In her imaginings of massed tree trunks, brush jumps, walls and ditches, the memory of Clover slipped to the back of her mind again; was almost forgotten.

"So you *must* wake Willow up, let her gallop on. She must keep up with Tarquin."

"And you," said Sally, "will need to control Tarquin. Not let him bash on out of control."

"Tarquin is never out of control . . ."

"Sally! Sally!" called Em's voice. "Where are you?"

Sally jumped to her feet, waving her arms above her head.

"Here," she yelled. "By the summer-house."

Em came racing towards them, first over the roughly-cut grass which they called the lawn and then through the long grass, her fair hair bannering behind her as she ran.

Misty, the Lorimers' grey and white bearded collie, leapt at Em's side, barking hysterically, her long coat flying out about her like a Chinese dragon's. Behind them both, Meg, the Lorimers' other beardie, panted to keep up. Meg was black and white. She was twelve years old, which Mrs Lorimer called a good age but really meant that she was getting old; more ready to lie on the ground and bark at a noise than go bustling and bounding to discover what was happening.

Sally could see Em's mouth opening and closing but she couldn't hear what she was saying because of Misty's noise.

"Shut it!" Sally yelled. "Belt up, Misty!"

"Flippin' beardies," exclaimed Em reaching Sally. "It's the phone for you.

14

Something about practising for the cross-country at the show."

Thalia sprang to her feet and grabbing Sally's hand raced her madly towards the house.

"Cross-country," she yelled. "A practice for the cross-country. That is just what we need."

Chapter Two

They ran through the kitchen, narrowly missing Sally's mother, and on into the hall. Sally picked up the receiver but her breathless hello was met with a humming silence.

"There's no one there," she said.

"Rubbish. There must be," declared Thalia. Grabbing the phone from Sally she yelled, "Hello! Hello! Hello!"

"Unfortunately," said Mr Lorimer, "telephones do not respond to shouting. If they've hung up, you have had it."

He took the receiver from Thalia, tried one hello of his own and hung up.

"She sounded young," said Em, skipping

into the kitchen. "About Sally's age."

"Didn't she say who she was?" cried Thalia.

"Uh, uh," said Em shaking her head. "Only something about the Pony Club."

"The Pony Club!" exclaimed Thalia. "Oh, you should have told them to hold on."

"I did," said Em, scowling at Thalia. "How was I to know you two would be at the back of beyond?"

"Whoever it was, they are quite certain to phone back," soothed Mrs Lorimer.

"I thought you would have been a founder member of the Pony Club?" asked Mr Lorimer.

"Well, no," said Thalia. "Well, actually no, because before you came to Kestrels I didn't want anyone to find out where I was keeping Tarquin. Some nosy Pony Club mum telling the police that I was keeping him here without permission and Tarquin would have had to live in Narg's tool shed. Not much room."

"While you were in prison for trespassing?" suggested Em.

"But of course," agreed Thalia. "I am humble and grateful for all I receive. So are Narg's spades and forks and clippers and shears and plant-pots for not having to share their home with a pony."

"OK, OK," said Mr Lorimer. "Grateful you may be but humble you are not and thank goodness for that."

Mrs Lorimer handed round crisps and lemonade and before they had finished drinking the phone rang again. Sally reached it first.

"Could I speak to Sally Lorimer?"

"Me," said Sally.

"Oh, good. I'm Verity Blair and Mum asked me to phone. We're having a practice for the cross-country events at Tarent Show. Martine Dawes told us that you had entered, so would you like to come?"

"Me too," breathed Thalia.

"When is it?" asked Sally, a mixture of excitement and nerves tingling her spine.

"Tomorrow. Eleven o'clock."

"Can I come too?" Thalia demanded, speaking into the phone.

"Are you the other girl who jumped the wall with Nick Ross?"

"Yes, on Tarquin."

"Then you're invited. Mum just didn't know where to find you. Here's Mum to speak to Sally's mother. See you tomorrow. Bye."

"That was Mrs Blair," said Mrs Lorimer when she had finished speaking on the phone.

"Then it is the Pony Club. Mrs Blair organises the Pony Club."

"We're all invited to go to their house tomorrow. Eleven o'clock. You two are to ride and we are to be support group. Apparently they have a cross-country course in their grounds which sounds very grand to me."

"And we've to jump it?" demanded Sally.

"Well, it sounded like it to me."

"Of course you've to jump," exclaimed Thalia in disgust. "You're jumping with me in five days, aren't you? I've told you, Willow will love it as long as you don't try to hold her back. Just keep her up with me!"

Before Sally had time to answer back the phone rang again.

"Martine Dawes," said Mr Lorimer when he had answered it. "She's taking a pony over to Ashdale – that's the Blair's house – for the practice tomorrow. A man is hiring a pony for the day for his son to ride and there will be room in the box for your two. She'll pick you up at ten. And she says although it won't be super-posh you had better look respectable."

"Well, of all the cheek," said Mrs Lorimer. "Sally always does."

"Don't worry, Mrs Lorimer," said Thalia. "She means me. Even when Narg does her very best I still look sort of tatty. Can't help it. It's my nature. Better start now – clean tack, wash hair and up at dawn to groom."

They were ready before ten the next morning, standing in the stable yard waiting for the sound of a horsebox turning down Kestrels' drive. Willow and Tarquin looked over the half-doors of their boxes, their coats gleaming, hoofs oiled and halters over their bridles.

"Should think we'll arrive just after you," said Mrs Lorimer who was waiting to see them off. "I've to pick up Narg. We're bringing a picnic."

The last thing I could possibly do is eat, thought Sally, but said nothing knowing that her mother would fuss.

"Here she is," shouted Thalia. They all heard the heavy rumble of a horsebox trundling down the drive.

They led their ponies out into the yard. Tarquin's head was held high on a giraffe neck, his nostrils wide, his ears sharp as he pranced at Thalia's side. Willow stood with her front hoofs set neatly together, her dark eyes bright, waiting calmly to see what was going to happen next.

Martine was driving and a boy who looked about ten or eleven was sitting next to her. He had straight blond hair that fell over his dark eyes. His shoulders were hunched forward and even when Martine jumped down from the cab he didn't look up, just sat looking down at his hands.

"Hi! Super day. Glad you're on time.

Let's get them on board. Have they been in a horsebox before?"

"Don't know," chorused Sally and Thalia.

"Soon find out," said Martine, lowering the ramp.

There was a chestnut pony tied at the far end of the box, held in place by a wooden bar.

"Dragonfly. For Simon to ride. Definitely, but definitely, *not* the pony I would have chosen for Simon to ride but once Mr Knowles starts shouting he usually gets what he wants. Now, lead Willow in first. Walk straight in. Don't let her stop."

Sally gulped. Then, leading Willow by her halter, she walked smartly up the ramp into the vast darkness of the box. Willow's ears flickered. She whinnied, a small questioning sound.

"It's all right," whispered Sally. "There's a good pony. On we go."

Willow's hoofs tip-tapped on the hollow-sounding ramp as she followed Sally obediently into the box.

"What a good pony," praised Martine, taking the halter rope from Sally and tying Willow up with a quick release knot. "Wish they were all like her," and Sally grinned with pride.

"Now Tarquin."

Thalia rushed Tarquin at the ramp.

"Steady," Martine warned. "Take it easy."

As they reached the ramp Tarquin reared up. He tossed his head, neighing wildly, making Mrs Lorimer back off to a safe distance. When he felt the wood under his front hoofs he spun round and, dragging Thalia, tried to canter off.

Martine sprang to grab Tarquin's bridle but Thalia was faster. Catching Tarquin's bit-ring she pulled his head round.

"Idiot," she told him. "Behave your bloomin' self. Get into the box."

And almost before Tarquin realised what was happening, Thalia was running him towards the ramp. At the exact moment when he was about to rear again Thalia slapped the halter rope hard on Tarquin's neck and roared at him to stop mucking about. With a huge leap Tarquin stormed into the box. By the time Martine reached Thalia she was praising her pony, feeding him with peppermints and telling him what a brave pony he was.

Martine regarded Thalia with raised eyebrows.

"Perhaps if you had taken things easier from the beginning?" she suggested.

"That wouldn't have worked," Thalia assured her. "You've got to be quick with Tarquin. He's not Willow."

"Well," said Martine, "your timing was spot on."

The horsebox rattled over the country roads to Ashdale. Martine drove with easy confidence. The boy whom Martine had introduced as Simon Knowles was squashed against the cab window while Sally balanced on Thalia's knee. Behind Thalia's head was a small window into the back of the box. Peering through it Sally could just make out the dim shapes of the ponies, the glint of the white of an eye, the arch of a neck and dust motes dazzling in a beam of light that sprayed over Willow's dappled quarters.

Sally swallowed hard. In less than an hour she would be galloping Willow at cross-country jumps. Suddenly her old fear gripped her – the fear of being thrown off Tarquin into the rusty nails of the breakwater; the dreadful moments when she was left behind when Willow jumped and she knew she would be thrown over Willow's head when she landed.

" 'Improved beyond belief'." Sally repeated Martine's praise to encourage herself. If only that man hadn't been shouting so much I could have heard her better . . . and Sally stopped short in mid-thought, for of course Simon Knowles, the boy sitting next to them in the cab, was the same boy. Vaguely Sally remembered that the man had been telling the boy that he must have a pony to ride on Monday.

And the pony he is to ride is Dragonfly from Mr Frazer's stables!

Sally twisted her head round so she

could get a better look at Simon. Totally ignoring Thalia's incessant chatter, he was staring determinedly out of the cab window.

"How long have you been in the Pony Club?" Sally asked him.

Simon twitched away from her words, turned his shoulder against her and went on staring at the passing scenery.

"Here we are," announced Martine as she drove past a high beech hedge, past wrought-iron gates and turned down a rutted lane that took them into the grounds of Ashdale. They went through a field gate to where several trailers were already parked and children were riding about.

"Out we get," organised Martine, jumping down from the cab.

Sally and Thalia squeezed over to the driving seat and leapt out. Simon sat still, ignoring them.

The ramp of the horsebox was lowered, Martine untied Tarquin who surged out of the box. Willow whinnied a welcome to Sally and stepped carefully down the ramp. Martine led out the prancing, chestnut pony.

"Where's Simon?" she demanded.

"Still in the cab," said Thalia.

"Tell him to come and take Dragonfly," said Martine, then hesitated. "No, don't bother. Here comes Mr Ronald Knowles in person. Cover up your earholes!"

"Simon! Simon!" roared a man's voice. "Come on. Waken up. NOW! At once. NOW! Get out of that box NOW! I'm not hiring that pony to have you sitting sleeping all day. Out, I tell you. OUT!"

Mr Knowles came striding towards the horsebox. To Sally he looked like a furious scarecrow. His bony wrists stuck out of his tweed jacket and his head with its bushy crop of short black hair burst out of his polo-necked sweater. All his jangling energy was aimed at Simon.

Sally swallowed hard, glad that Mr Knowles was not her father.

Simon opened the cab door and slid to the ground without looking at his father.

"I do not know," said Martine aloud, to herself, "why he won't leave Simon alone. Poor kid, having him to cope with as well as everything else."

Chapter Three

"Hello. I'm Verity Blair," said a dark-haired girl with glasses and rosy cheeks, riding up to Sally on a thick-set bay pony. "I phoned you up. We're all very glad you could come. Mum's always desperate to find new members for the Pony Club. We're such a squidgy wee branch."

"Oh," said Sally, wondering if Verity's mother would still be glad to see her if she fell off Willow. Sally could see what looked like the first two jumps of the cross-country course – two telegraph poles and then a brush jump.

Sally's heart sank. Really she hadn't done any cross-country jumping. The red and white poles in the paddock of Mr Frazer's riding school seemed suddenly quite safe compared to galloping over rough ground where rabbit burrows or loose stones might bring Willow to her knees. Just as her imagination was taking over, transforming the small Pony Club size obstacles into Badminton fences, Sally remembered the unicorn lying in her pocket. She took it out and it sparkled in the palm of her hand.

"I'm Thalia Nisbet," announced Thalia. "You said I was to come too."

"Oh, yes. Mum knew you lived some-where round here but she could never find out where. We called you the vanishing rider."

"Well, here I am now. Can we see the jumps?" said Thalia, quickly changing the subject.

"Over this way," said Verity turning her pony and leading the way out of the field. They rode along a lane and through an open gate to a stretch of rough country.

"Whee!" enthused Thalia. "Super!" and

standing up in her stirrups she gazed round at a course of about fifteen obstacles.

There were the first two jumps that Sally had seen from the field then the course followed a track through bracken, then down a slope that seemed to Sally as steep as a playground slide and on over a stream and a wall, finishing with a spread of tin drums.

"Don't worry," said Verity, seeing Sally's stricken expression. "That's the full course. We'll only be jumping a few of them. Mum is madly cautious."

"But I want to jump them all!" exclaimed Thalia. "Could I have a go now?"

"No you could not. I'm not even allowed to ride round it unless it's official."

"But no one would know," said Thalia, and to Sally's horror she began to gather in her reins ready to ride over the obstacles.

"Oh yes they would," said Verity. "Here they come." But she was smiling, her eyes dancing at Thalia's daring.

Thalia looked back over her shoulder and saw nine ponies and riders led by Mrs Blair on foot, coming out of the lane. Behind them were about twenty parents and friends including Sally's mother and Thalia's narg.

"Glory gosh," said Thalia. "Good job I didn't. Narg would have splattered me."

"But you would have gone round, wouldn't you?" asked Verity.

"Would," said Thalia.

"Everybody, everybody," called Mrs Blair clapping her hands, rallying her ride. "Make a wide circle and we'll school to begin with. Pony's length apart, Walk on. Good striding walk."

They heard Mr Knowles before they saw him.

"I told you you would be last. Always last. What's happened to you, boy? Think you couldn't ride. Get on with you. Thirty pounds it cost me to hire that pony, so get riding!"

They burst out of the leafy shelter of the lane, Dragonfly at a ragged trot, Simon sitting loosely in the saddle, his head turned away from his father who was running at his side shouting.

"Simon, slot in behind Blackbird," said Mrs Blair. "That's it."

"RIDE BOY! RIDE!" bawled Mr Knowles.

There was an indrawn breath of irritation from the spectators; tongues tutting as they turned to speak to each other.

"Wake him up," roared Mr Knowles as Simon rode round making no attempt to control Dragonfly.

"Prepare to halt. Halt," commanded Mrs Blair and she marched straight up to Mr Knowles.

"If you cannot be quiet kindly go back to your car and leave Simon with me."

"The lad's a wimp . . ." began Mr Knowles.

"If you please," insisted Mrs Blair.

She was short, thick-set with large flat eyes that glared up at Mr Knowles waiting until his six foot height turned unwillingly away to join the other parents.

Sally looked across the circle at Simon.

If her father had ever behaved like that she would have died, wanted the earth to open and swallow her up, but Simon was totally ignoring all the commotion. He was staring out over the hills while the chestnut Dragonfly fretted at his bit.

"Prepare to walk. Walk on," said Mrs Blair.

Two middle-aged ladies crossed the field close to the ride and as Sally rode past she heard one lady say to the other:

"Tragic, really tragic. When you think what it all used to be like."

"And Simon! He used to be such a super rider and now . . ."

"Sorry dear, sorry," said the other lady catching Mrs Blair's hard stare and they both scuttled off to join the other parents.

"Prepare to trot. Trot on," called Mrs Blair giving Sally no time to think about what she had overheard.

After they had schooled at a walk, trot and canter Mrs Blair took them down to where there were four cross-country obstacles – two jumps made out of barrels, one with a pole on the far side, a dry stone wall and a post and rails. They took it in turn to jump.

Willow popped neatly over all four jumps taking them at a slow, steady canter and Sally managed to stay with her pony, making her feel fizzy with success. She rode back to the others clapping Willow's neck and praising her.

Tarquin plunged and soared over the jumps.

"High flier!" exclaimed Mrs Blair but didn't stop to listen to Thalia's explanations.

"Is that everyone? Everyone had a turn?"

"Simon!" roared Mr Knowles and Simon who had been hiding at the back of the other riders walked reluctantly forward.

"Please Simon," said Mrs Blair speaking directly to Simon who had turned his head away from her. "Do stop this silly nonsense. Now let me see you jumping. I know Dragonfly, he'll take you over these obstacles without a second thought."

Simon gathered his reins together and

trotted Dragonfly in a circle. He turned towards the first jump and Dragonfly broke into a gallop, pounding up to the jump. At exactly the point where Dragonfly would have taken off Simon pulled his pony to one side, forcing him to canter round the side of the jump.

"What on earth is he doing?" asked Thalia.

"He stopped him! He did it on purpose," said Sally. "Perhaps he's afraid of jumping."

But Simon did not look scared. His face was set in a bleak mask of determination.

"There," he said riding back to Mrs Blair. "I've jumped. That's it."

Mrs Blair stepped towards him, opening her mouth as if she was going to speak, then quite suddenly she stopped and came back to stand in front of the other riders.

"You all jumped well," she said. "Now everyone is going to go round again and I want to see you letting your ponies gallop on. Canter a circle first and then ride the jumps as a course. Let your ponies go on, taking the jumps in their stride. You are thinking of the whole course, not of four single jumps. Verity, take Buster round first. Remember to look up and think ahead."

Verity cantered in a wide circle, turned to the first jump and let her pony gallop on.

Watching intently Sally could see the difference in the way Verity was riding. As she landed from the first jump she was looking ahead to the second jump, riding on without hesitation.

Tarquin scorched round and Mrs Blair said if he touched a fixed jump at that speed he would come down and she made Thalia jump again steadying Tarquin to a canter.

"You see, he can jump perfectly well at that speed," said Mrs Blair. "It is up to you to control him."

When it was Sally's turn she could still picture Verity's round, how she had urged her pony on, riding smoothly, without hesitation, but when Sally came to the first jump she just couldn't stop herself steadying Willow to a collected canter, letting her pop neatly over the jump and then when she had landed safely, ride her at the next jump doing exactly the same thing.

"Don't be afraid, dear," said Mrs Blair sympathetically. "You must have confidence in your pony. She'll jump for you."

"We're jumping in the pairs at the show," interrupted Thalia.

"Really," said Mrs Blair as if she did not think it was a good idea.

This time Simon did not try to jump. Neither Mrs Blair nor his father paid any attention to him and when Mrs Blair led the way to the cross-country course Simon dragged behind at the end of the ride.

In spite of Thalia's pleading Mrs Blair only let them tackle five of the obstacles.

"But you saw him," pleaded Thalia. "You saw how he sailed over them. Please let me jump them all."

"Yes, I saw you and you must steady him up," said Mrs Blair sharply. "School him at a sitting trot over cavaletti."

Thalia groaned and muttered.

Willow jumped the poles, the gorse fence and the barrels with Sally sitting balanced in the saddle. At the ditch and pole she was left behind and Willow stopped at the next jump, waited until Sally got herself sorted out, then jumped it easily the second time.

"Not at all bad," said Mrs Blair. "Don't be afraid to let Willow canter on. She'll jump if she possibly can. It was your fault that she stopped at the last jump. You were left behind. I think from the way she jumps she's been round a cross-country course before this. She'll look after you."

Sally nodded, knowing that what Mrs Blair said was true. It was her fault. She hadn't let Willow gallop on.

"And if you are jumping in the pairs with Thalia, she is going to have to slow down and you must speed up. You'll both need to put in some hard work before the show. School together as a pair and then practise over broad, easy jumps, concentrating on keeping together as a pair."

Sally felt her heart sink. She was sure

she would never dare to keep up with Thalia. For a second her old fear of being run away with lit up in her mind – Willow charging madly over rough hillside, crashing into jumps or falling while she sat helplessly, totally out of control.

Stop it. Stop it at once, Sally told herself. That's all past. Willow won't run away with you, and she clapped Willow's solid shoulder and smoothed down her silver mane. If she was riding Willow she was safe.

"Does Simon want to jump?" asked Mrs Blair when everyone else had been round the course.

"He'll jump," stated Mr Knowles running up to Simon and slapping Dragonfly on the quarters, flinging his arms wide to chase the pony on.

Before Mrs Blair could do anything Dragonfly had burst into a ragged canter and was charging up the hillside while Simon sat, close as a limpet, his face expressionless.

Seeing the telegraph poles in front of

him and remembering how he had been pulled aside from the other jumps the chestnut pony pricked his ears, snatched at his bit and charged at the telegraph poles.

"Jump it," roared Mr Knowles "Jump!"

Instantly Simon shortened his reins. Pulling with all his strength on his left rein he fought to stop Dragonfly reaching the jump.

The pony reared up in temper, struggling to free his head. He touched down and bucked wildly but Simon, still looking as if nothing was happening, dug in his right heel tight and hard and jerked on the left rein, forcing Dragonfly to avoid the jump. The pony, pulled off balance, staggered and nearly fell.

"He'll end up killing the boy," said Martine Dawes as she watched Simon. "Wait till I tell Mr Frazer about this."

"Why won't his father leave him alone?" demanded a watching father. "The boy does not want to jump. That is obvious."

"Well, he will *not* be hiring another

pony from us," answered Martine. "Not if I have anything to do with it."

Dragonfly careered over the hillside, a bright flying shape, completely out of control with Simon sitting easily in the saddle.

"Simon, come back at once," called Mrs Blair groaning despairingly. "Simon, come back!"

But Simon showed no sign of hearing her.

"Would you take the ride over?" Mrs Blair asked Martine.

Martine nodded and began organising ponies and riders back to the field.

Twisting round in her saddle, Sally saw Mrs Blair march briskly towards Simon; saw Simon bring Dragonfly to a walk and, turning, begin to ride back down the hill. When Sally lost sight of them Mrs Blair was standing beside them, her hand on Dragonfly's neck, talking earnestly to Simon.

Chapter Four

By nine o'clock the next morning, Thalia
and Sally were riding between the beech
trees down the long drive from Kestrels.
They were going to find obstacles to
jump. Before they had left Ashdale
Mrs Blair, talking to all the children,
had told them that between now and
the show they were to pop their ponies
over anything small that could be jumped
– a low place in a hedge, a dry stone wall,
a fallen tree trunk – anything natural that
their ponies would be able to jump easily.
Anything to get them used to jumping
strange obstacles that they hadn't seen
before.

Mrs Blair had also talked about schooling at a sitting trot and jumping three low poles set in a schooling circle.

Thalia only remembered the jumping.

They rode across the sand dunes and over the shore to the rotting breakwater.

"Mrs Blair said we were to look carefully before we jumped," cautioned Sally. "Make sure that the landing is OK."

"Not here," shouted Thalia, riding Tarquin at the breakwater. "We know it's OK here."

"I was only telling you what Mrs Blair said," insisted Sally, but Thalia was already jumping the breakwater.

Sally gathered Willow together and jumped behind her.

"Now," organised Thalia. "We'll trot a circle, ride at it together and jump as a pair. Right?"

They trotted a circle, turned towards the breakwater and instantly Tarquin tore at the jump, his racing hoofs winged with sand. He had landed far out on the other side before Willow had taken off.

They jumped three more times and each time the same thing happened.

"We are meant to be a pair!" exclaimed Thalia. "I am not meant to be giving you a lead."

"Then don't," snapped Sally. "Keep him back with me. Willow won't go racing at a jump like an idiot, the way you do."

For a moment they stared at each other, on the edge of fighting.

It was Thalia who took off her hard hat, shook out her sunburst of hair and laughed.

"Let's find something else to jump," she said. "Tarquin knows ye ancient old breakwaters too well. He's too used to belting over them. Let's go and ask Mr Palmer if we can jump over his farm land. He's friendly enough with Narg so I should think he'd let us."

But even when they had permission to ride on Mr Palmer's land they couldn't find much to jump. They had just finished dragging two empty hen coops into the middle of a field when Mrs Palmer appeared at the field gate, yelling at them to put the coops back where they belonged.

"Not our bloomin' day," muttered Thalia when they were riding away from the farm.

"Where are we going now?" asked Sally, thinking that perhaps they should go home and school as a pair over the jumps in the field.

"Sandwiches," stated Thalia.

They found a track leading over the hillside and rode along it until they came to a clear peaty stream. They dismounted, loosened their girths and let the ponies drink. Then they sat down on the boulders at the side of the water, arms through their grazing ponies' reins and ate their sandwiches.

White clouds drifted over clear blue sky. Far above them the soaring silhouette of a buzzard rose and fell on thermals of air.

Why can't we just enjoy ourselves, Sally thought. It's all perfect the way it is. Ponies and being happy. If it wasn't for this jumping we could just be here. Willow's enormous head loomed over her shoulder searching for titbits.

"We could just stay here," Sally said aloud.

"I've thought," Thalia announced, springing to her feet, ignoring Sally. "We'll ride up to the Moss. There's plenty of stone walls there. Masses at the right height for us to practise over as a pair."

As Sally tugged up Willow's girth and mounted she knew there was something she had heard about the Moss, some warning about riding there, but she couldn't quite remember what it was.

"We can go on along this track," said Thalia riding on confidently. "I don't know why I didn't think about the Moss before," and she glanced out of the corner of her eye at Sally, checking to see what she was thinking.

They followed the track for about half an hour, then rode along a broader tree-lined path.

"Nearly there," said Thalia as they left the lane. Spreading out before them was a wide reach of flat, open land. On their left was a stretch of water overgrown with reeds. Whitewashed farmhouses were scattered about the sloping green fields and on their right was the garden of a stone-built bungalow with two looseboxes and an overgrown paddock.

Thalia trotted ahead until they passed the garden and rough grazing criss-crossed by dry stone walls took its place.

"Super!" gasped Sally. "What a smashing place to ride. Why have we never come here before?"

But Thalia didn't answer. She was already cantering over the grass and jumping Tarquin over a low wall.

"You can jump where you like," shouted Thalia. "Come on."

At first Sally checked cautiously, peering over walls to make sure there were no fallen stones on the landing side but even when Willow's hoofs clattered on fallen stones it didn't seem to make any difference to her; she never felt like falling. Thalia's recklessness, Willow's pricked ears and dancing hoofs filled Sally with delight. She completely forgot her fears and like Thalia galloped over the small fields, leaping over the walls in an ecstasy of freedom.

"There's a better wall further on," said Thalia, her eyes bright; Tarquin's arched neck and stamping hoofs demanding more galloping, more jumping. "Down this way."

They rode down the hillside to the track, Willow following Tarquin, making high pig squeals of excitement. When they reached the track Thalia let Tarquin gallop on until they reached a stone wall that ran between the track and the water. It was about two feet high. The land between the wall and the water was short, rough grazing.

"You can jump it anywhere," cried Thalia as she swung Tarquin off the track to the right and turned him to jump the wall.

But Sally didn't follow her. There was something not right about the ground on the other side. Somehow the grass looked too smooth, too bright.

Tarquin plunged at the wall. Sally saw him soar out and land. Only he didn't land. He sank through the ground, his legs vanishing instantly; his belly, chest and quarters sinking more slowly out of sight.

Sally's cries mingled with Tarquin's high, terrible screaming.

In a split second Thalia had torn off her anorak, thrown it across the grass towards the wall and squirming her legs free from the bog had launched herself on to it and with a convulsive struggle had reached the firm ground by the wall. Her left hand was clenched on to the buckle of Tarquin's reins.

"Get help! Get help!" she cried but already Sally was galloping full out, back to the bungalow. As she bent low over Willow's neck she could see nothing but Tarquin's reaching neck, bursting eyeballs and screaming nostrils.

A wicker gate in the garden hedge was open. Sally stormed through it, galloped to the door and falling from Willow pressed her finger on the bell and kept it there.

To Sally's utter astonishment it was Mr Knowles who came to the door.

"What the . . ." he began.

"There's a pony in the swamp. He's right in up to his neck. Quick! Quick! You've got to do something at once."

A grey-haired woman in a floral dress had followed Mr Knowles to the door.

"I'll phone Alan Campbell," she said. "Get him to bring his tractor and a rope. Please God he's in."

Sally was leaning against the door post, tears pouring down her face.

In minutes the woman was back.

"He's coming at once," she said. "We'd better get to them."

She ran across the garden and picked up a bike that was leaning against a garden seat.

Simon was standing at the foot of the stairs. Sally did not know how long he had been there, what he had heard.

"A tractor's no use," he said urgently.

"It'll sink. You've got to get a JCB. There's one ditching at Carruth Farm."

But Mr Knowles rushed past him and Sally, too, turned Willow and springing on to her galloped back to Thalia and Tarquin.

When Sally reached them the floral lady had her arm round Thalia's shoulders. Like some weird statue Tarquin's head and neck were still above the swamp ground and Thalia's hand was still tightly clenched on Tarquin's reins.

Mr Knowles reached them next carrying a rough rope halter and blankets.

"Still with us?" he asked, staring at Tarquin's head. "Looks as if he's got his feet on to a bank of firm ground. All depends how long that will hold."

Thalia's face was clenched shut, all her will centred on Tarquin.

"Here," said Mr Knowles tossing the rope halter to Thalia. "You're the lightest. Lie down flat where your anorak is and see if you can get this round his head. They'll never pull him out by those reins."

Thalia lay flat on the ground, the floral lady holding one foot, Mr Knowles the other, and began to squirm over her anorak towards Tarquin. He rolled his eyes and laid back his ears as Thalia lassoed the halter over his head and with shaking hands managed to tie a knot in it. Then holding tightly on to the rope Thalia was pulled back to firm ground.

They waited in silence, trying not to stare at Tarquin but hardly able to take their eyes off him.

"The tractor!" cried Thalia, her skinned ears hearing it first.

And with its huge wheels rumbling over the rough track the tractor bounced towards them.

"Who got the bloomin' horse stuck in there?" demanded Alan Campbell driving right up to them, jumping down. "If you bloomin' kids would keep off my land. How often have you been told that it's too swampy to ride on it?"

He took the rope from Thalia and going as close to Tarquin as he could he tried to pull at his head but with no effect.

"Can't do anything from here," he said, dragging his boots free from the swamp, and coming back to them.

"Need to try and get down closer to him. See if I can get a pull on him from there. He's bloomin' deep. Don't know if I can do anything."

Alan Campbell backed his tractor to the end of the wall, turned it to drive off the track and for a second the giant wheels advanced over the bright grass then sank slowly into the swamp and he was held prisoner as fatally as Tarquin.

They all stared at the stationary tractor in fascinated horror. What could they do now? A dry, cracked sound came from the base of Thalia's throat and she began to shake uncontrollably.

Sally staring at Tarquin was sure she saw his neck sink deeper into the swamp.

The adults talked in quick, desperate voices. Mr Knowles got on the bike to go and phone the police. The floral lady tried to wrap a blanket round Thalia and Sally bit hard on her knuckles to stop herself screaming. She could not believe that this nightmare was real.

There was a clonking and shuddering that shook the ground, startling them all, as down the track came a JCB.

Thalia shook herself free from the floral lady's blanket. She sprang to her feet.

"He's here," she cried. "Oh, quick, quick. Hurry."

The man driving the JCB was tall, broad shouldered with a mop of white curls. He jolted to a shuddering halt and, sucking through his teeth, sized up the situation. He exchanged a few muttered words with the young man who was with him. The young man climbed into the bucket at the end of the JCB's long crane arm and was swung out above Tarquin's head.

No one spoke. They all watched in terrified silence as the young man hooked up the halter rope. He fixed it securely to the JCB and inch by desperate inch the JCB began to winch Tarquin from the swamp.

At first only his head and neck moved, they were stretched out as Tarquin was dragged forward. Sally was sure that the rope would snap, Thalia certain that Tarquin's neck would be broken.

Relentlessly the JCB dragged Tarquin forward. His shoulders burst free from the swamp but he gave no sign of life. For minutes that seemed like hours, like days, they watched Tarquin being dragged forward until at last he lay on solid ground, a huge bulk of swamped pony.

Thalia, who had never taken her eyes off Tarquin for a second, threw herself down at Tarquin's head. She crouched beside him pulling his ears through her hands, whispering his name, talking to him, but for minutes he lay without any sign of life, and then his ear twitched.

"He's not dead," cried Thalia. "He's not dead!" Almost as if he had understood her words Tarquin surged to his feet, stood uncertainly, then shook himself, gobbets of swamp flying from him. Then to everyone's absolute delight he took a few steps forward and began to graze as if nothing had happened.

"How on earth did you know we were here?" Mr Knowles asked the JCB driver.

"A boy phoned Carruth. Bob came out shouting that it was urgent so I came straight away. Not the first beast I've pulled out of that bog. Bloomin' dangerous place."

Thalia threw muddied arms round his neck and kissed him.

"Now I know," she said, "what the angel Gabriel will look like."

"It was Simon who phoned," stated Sally. "He said we needed a JCB, that a tractor would be no use. But no one paid any attention to him."

"Where is he now?" barked Mr Knowles. "Skulking in the house. Should have been out here giving us a hand. Useless boy!"

They went back to the Knowles' bungalow while Mr Knowles phoned Kestrels and arranged with a horrified Mrs Lorimer about paying for the tractor and the JCB. Thalia and Sally tried to wash some of the swamp off Tarquin in the yard, drank the hot sweet tea the floral lady had made for them and thanked Mr Knowles.

"I must thank Simon too," Thalia insisted. "He thought of the JCB. I've got to thank him."

But Mr Knowles had turned back to the house without answering Thalia. The floral lady said not to worry, that she would see Simon.

The girls left the bungalow by the side gate, Sally riding Willow and Thalia leading Tarquin.

"You would think he might have called Simon so I could have thanked him," said Thalia.

Her face was chalk-white and she walked with an arm over Tarquin's withers who, in spite of his ordeal, was walking along without any sign of lameness, his eyes bright and his face alert.

From one of the upstairs windows of the bungalow a boy looked down at them

– straight wing of blond hair, dark eyes and fixed, unyielding mouth.

"Simon!" yelled Thalia waving her arms. "Come down. I want to thank you. Thank you for saving Tarquin."

But with a twitch of the curtain Simon had gone.

"Why didn't he come down?" demanded Sally.

"Too late now," said Thalia. "That motorbike you can hear is Narg coming to find out what's been happening. There is going to be dire distress."

Chapter Five

Thalia was right. There was dire distress, both from her narg and Sally's parents. Words like foolish, irresponsible and stupid were used a lot and in the end they had to promise never to jump over anything unless there was an adult with them or the jump was on Kestrels' ground and had been seen by Mr or Mrs Lorimer.

"Never?" cried Thalia in dismay.

"Well, not until you are much older," warned her narg.

Next morning when Thalia led Tarquin round the field he was still perfectly sound.

"I'll come over when I'm back from the dentist's torture chamber," she announced.

"Be about four. They can both have a day of rest."

Left alone Sally was bored. She brushed the beardies and tidied her bedroom then hung about the kitchen pestering her mother.

"We're going shopping," said Mrs Lorimer, holding Jamie by one hand and shopping bags in the other. "Are you coming?"

"Ice cream," said Jamie. "I'm having spider flavour. There's dead fly, squashed worm or mouse tail."

Sally resisted the temptation.

When they had gone she wandered down to the ponies' field again and leant on the gate watching them grazing.

The nightmare picture of Tarquin vanishing into the swamp was still vivid in her mind.

If Simon hadn't phoned for the JCB it would have been too late. Too late for any of us to have phoned. By that time Tarquin would have been swallowed up by the swamp, she thought, and shuddered, remembering clearly how she had seen Tarquin's neck sinking deeper into the bog.

Although Sally had agreed with Thalia that it would be a good idea to give the ponies a rest day she decided that it wouldn't do Willow any harm to ride her along the beach – just for half an hour at the walk.

She took Meg with her and rode slowly along the shore thinking about Simon – the strange way he wouldn't jump; didn't seem to want to ride at all and yet when Dragonfly had been galloping and bucking his way over the hillside Simon had stayed on effortlessly.

Sally tried to remember what the women had said to each other. Something about it all being tragic.

Tragic? Sally thought, wondering what could have happened to Simon. So bad a thing that people called it tragic.

Meg trotted along beside Willow carrying a lump of driftwood in her mouth.

"You are the best dog," Sally told her.

"The best dog in the world," and Meg looked up at her, smiling with her eyes, wagging her tail.

Sally had never known life without Meg. Meg had been three when Sally was born. She had always been there. Last year she would have been racing over the beach, digging in the sand, rolling in the seaweed, chasing gulls, but now her good age had slowed her down, clouded her eyes and stiffened her joints. Sally swallowed hard and steadied Willow to a halt. Meg dropped her lump of wood and sat down panting, glad of the rest.

The tide was far out, the wet sands gleaming. Sally touched her reins and let Willow walk on towards a black castle of rock, close to the sea's edge. Meg picked up her driftwood and followed behind.

They had almost reached the mass of rock when Meg ran on ahead, her barking muffled through her lump of wood. She went right up to the rock, dropped the driftwood and stepped back barking furiously, asking whoever was there to throw it for her.

Sally screwed up her eyes against the sun but could see no one. She shouted to Meg to behave herself and rode towards the rock. There, sitting hidden by a cleft in the rock, staring out to sea, was a boy with straight blond hair.

"Simon!" Sally exclaimed in amazement. "Why are you here?" and then realising that it wasn't any of her business she shouted at Meg to be quiet.

"Anyway," she went on. "I'm very glad you are here. We want to thank you for yesterday. For phoning for the JCB. You saved Tarquin."

Simon took Meg's lump of wood, threw it out to sea and Meg ran after it.

"It's OK," said Simon, still not looking at Sally. "I remembered last time when they were trying to get a sheep out. The tractor got stuck and the sheep went down. Even when you know the Moss well it's dangerous. Dad's getting the farmer to put up warning notices."

"But *you* remembered. *You* phoned the farm. It was *you* who saved Tarquin."

Meg dumped her driftwood back at Simon's feet and as he bent down to throw it for her again Sally saw that his face was streaked with tears. Obviously Simon had come out here to be alone. She thought of riding away, saying goodbye and pretending that she hadn't noticed – but she couldn't. Simon must be really miserable to be sitting here alone crying.

"What's wrong?" Sally asked, sliding down from Willow. "Can we help – that's Thalia and me. We'd both do anything to help because of you saving Tarquin. Honestly, anything."

Simon turned his head away.

"I don't need help," he said, but in the next second he had dropped his head on to his hands and was crying bitterly.

Sally waited, fiddling with Willow's mane until Simon had stopped crying, dried his eyes and blown his nose.

"Sorry. Didn't mean to carry on like that. Just everything's so hopeless. Dad shouting like an idiot all the time. But I don't care. I am never going to jump again. Not ever."

"Are you scared?" asked Sally sympathetically. "Before I got Willow I was scared of galloping and even now I'm not all that good at jumping."

"Course I'm not scared," said Simon. "I've won cups and lashings of rosettes. But it makes sense, doesn't it, when you've killed your pony and broken your legs you don't want to go and do the same thing again, do you? That makes sense, doesn't it?"

"Did you?" demanded Sally, hardly able to take in what Simon had told her.

"I was riding in hunter trials, going too fast because I had to catch up on time. I knew it was risky but I was sure Merlin could do it. And he could have, but he slipped on the take off. His leg got caught up on the fixed poles. He broke it and I came off and broke both of mine. They took me to hospital but they shot him. When they patched my bones together and they let me go home, all Dad would do was shout at me to ride again. At first I wouldn't ride at all. Then I gave in and rode at Pony Club things, on Mr Frazer's ponies. But that wasn't enough. Now it's shout, shout, shout at me to jump. You heard him. But I'm not. I'm not."

"Dragonfly nearly did," said Sally.

Simon nodded, shivering suddenly.

"Mr Frazer said that he wasn't letting Dad hire any more of his ponies; that I was ruining them. So now Dad's going to buy one. I can't stop him. That's where we should be today, only I managed to dodge out and come here."

"But don't you want a pony?" asked Sally in amazement. "Even when I was having nightmares about galloping I still wanted a pony!"

"Not the kind of pony Dad will buy. It will be a crazy chestnut like that Dragonfly. Wanting to do nothing else but jump and jump. It'll always be there in Merlin's box, reminding me of Merlin and some day it will all happen again. I know it will."

"What about your mum?"

"That was Aunt Dot you saw yesterday. Mum was killed in a car crash about a month before my fall," said Simon, his voice flat and distant as an old recording that had been played over and over again.

"Oh," said Sally, having no words; understanding what the women had meant by tragic.

"So you see we're a has been family."

"But if you had a pony like Willow," said Sally, returning to the only bit of Simon's story that she really understood.

"I just do not want a pony. Anyway Dad wouldn't buy a quiet sensible pony. He wants to see me back at the top."

"Bet you he would," said Sally. "Bet if you said that you'd ride a quiet pony he would buy one for you just so you would start riding again."

Simon shrugged his shoulders. "Where would he find one to buy? It's the show on Saturday. He knows about this pony that's fast and a brilliant jumper. That's the one we were going to see," and Simon sat staring out to sea, ignoring Meg's barking demand to throw her driftwood; ignoring Sally and Willow; staring hopelessly in front of him.

Although Simon had said he wasn't scared Sally thought he was. Not nervous the way she was but afraid to jump again after his smash. If he had a quiet pony, she thought, a pony that was his own, he would get to know her, would start riding again because he wanted to and that would be a beginning.

The noise Sally made was something like a hundred express trains coming out of a hundred tunnels. It made Meg bark more furiously than ever; it made the gulls at the sea's edge flock up in clamorous clouds; made Willow start and Simon jump to his feet.

"But of course," cried Sally. "You can buy Clover. She wouldn't jump! Not in a million years. Clover would be just the pony for you!"

Chapter Six

"Yes, I still have Clover," said Miss Meek's voice from the other end of the phone. "Yes, I suppose she is still for sale. Why? Have you changed your mind?"

"Not for me," said Sally. "Someone else. Could they come out tomorrow afternoon to see her? And could I come out in the morning with a friend to posh her up a bit?"

"Well," said Miss Meek in a surprised voice. "I suppose you could. We'd all love to see you again."

"Now," said Sally, going back to the living room where her family and Thalia were waiting to hear the result of her

70

phone call. "Miss Meek will be pleased to see us and Clover is still for sale."

At first Simon had insisted that he did not want any kind of pony.

"But if your father says that you must have one why not buy Clover? I promise you she is totally, one hundred per cent jump proof. Nothing would make Clover run away. Absolutely nothing would make her jump. At least persuade your father to go and see her."

"If you can fix it I'll go and look at her," Simon had said at last, getting to his feet, throwing Meg's driftwood for the last time. "Honestly I do not want a pony. I do not want to ride but I suppose it would make life easier if I do."

Yet as he walked away he had called back over his shoulder, "See you tomorrow," and had grinned at Sally, a sudden smile lighting up his bleak face.

"Now," said Sally, standing behind her father's chair and wrapping her arms round his neck. "It's your turn."

When Sally's parents had heard the story of Simon's accident they had both agreed that Clover would be a quiet, steady pony for him and Mr Lorimer had reluctantly agreed to phone up Mr Knowles telling him that he knew of a suitable pony for his son.

"Sound horsy," encouraged Mrs Lorimer as her husband got to his feet. "A man who knows a good horse when he sees one."

"I'll speak to him if you like," offered Thalia, but Sally was already dialling Simon's number.

Simon answered.

"It's Sally. Dad is here to speak to your father. Clover is still for sale."

"A thoroughly decent pony. Totally trustworthy. Just the thing for your son," Mr Lorimer assured Mr Knowles, while Mrs Lorimer buried her face in a cushion to stop her giggling being heard at the other end of the phone.

"They're coming to see Clover tomorrow afternoon about three. He was a bit suspicious about Miss Meek's riding school. Said he'd never heard of it. But I talked him round," Mr Lorimer told them, feeling pleased with himself.

Next morning Mr Lorimer gave Sally and Thalia a lift to the riding school on his way to work. They had been up early and practised jumping as a pair in the paddock but really it had not been jumping together, more Tarquin giving Willow a lead over the jumps.

"Hope they buy her," said Mr Lorimer before he drove away. "I'd like to see her in a good home. Always felt it was a bit miserable turning her down like that. Anyway, good luck," and he drove away to his library.

"Pretty grot," said Thalia looking round at Miss Meek's bungalow, stabling and the fields wired off into grazing strips. "Is that the lane where you rode? Wasn't it deadly boring?"

"Suppose so," said Sally, realising how much she had changed; how incredibly lucky she was to have all the freedom of Kestrels and Willow to ride.

Quickly Sally crossed the yard, peering into familiar stalls and boxes. Well-loved faces looked out over half-doors or turned in their stalls to see her – Tansy, Mint, Amber, Prince and Princess. Sally fed them sliced carrots from the bag she had brought with her, scratched necks, clapped shoulders, but Clover wasn't there.

"Must be out," said Sally and they ran round the stabling to the grazing strips.

"Clover," called Sally. "Clover!"

The black pony with the white socks was nibbling at the short grass with her rump turned towards Sally.

"Clover!" she called again and this time Clover heard her and swung round. She stood for a moment, her ears curious, her eyes questioning, and then with a welcoming whinny she trotted straight up to Sally.

"She knows me! She remembered me!" cried Sally throwing her arms over Clover's rough neck and straggling mane. "She knew it was me!"

"She's not much to look at," said Thalia critically. "D'you think Mr Knowles will want to buy her?"

"He MUST," insisted Sally. "He absolutely must."

Now that she had seen Clover again Sally could not bear the thought of leaving her behind in the riding school for a second time. Even if she did look a bit poor and overworked she would be the best possible pony for Simon. Clover would never jump and that was what Simon wanted.

Miss Meek asked them in for lemonade and biscuits. She questioned Sally about Kestrels and Willow. Thalia told her about Tarquin. Then Miss Meek asked them about the family who were interested in Clover.

"They've got two looseboxes and the boy who will ride her is a very good rider. He just wants a pony to ride around on. She would have a really good home," Sally told her.

"Wish someone would give me a really good home," said Miss Meek, setting her empty coffee mug on the table and standing up. "But seeing that is not likely to happen I'd better get on and do some work. You can bring Clover in and brush her down. You'll still remember where the brushes are kept?"

Clover stood like a wooden horse in the centre of the box while Sally and Thalia brushed out her mane and tail, washed her white socks and worked on her coat with a dandy brush until it was nearly shining.

As she groomed, the lump in Sally's throat grew bigger. She *so* wanted Clover to go home with Simon; she could not bear the thought of her being left at Miss Meek's.

"There," said Thalia, standing back and looking at Clover, "not quite a silk purse but less of a sow's ear. Let's eat."

Thalia refilled the water bucket and when Clover had finished drinking Sally tipped a feed of pony nuts which she had brought from Kestrels into Clover's manger. Then they sat outside, leaning against the box door eating their sandwiches and waiting for Simon.

Mr Knowles' low-slung, scarlet sports car swept into the yard pulling a single pony trailer behind it and instantly everything in the yard seemed shabbier, more rundown than ever. Simon was sitting next to his father staring out of the car window with his usual withdrawn air. Aunt Dot sat in the back.

"Hi," called Thalia jumping up and racing towards the car. "We've got Clover ready for you and thank you, thank you, thank you for saving Tarquin. Thank you, thank you for thinking of the JCB. Absolutely any time you want to ride Tarquin he is yours."

Simon shrugging his way out of the car said it was OK, while his father got out and stared round the yard.

"Some dump this," he shouted.

And Sally knew that Miss Meek must have heard him as she came across the yard towards them.

"We forgot to clean the tack," whispered Thalia as Miss Meek saddled and bridled Clover with a dry cracked bridle and sweated saddle.

But when Clover was led out of the box she didn't look too old or too thin. A sudden burst of sunlight made her eyes gleam and her coat shimmer. So for a moment she almost looked like the kind of pony that Mr Knowles might buy for his son. Almost.

"Well if it's an old scarecrow like this that you want to ride let's see you on it. SIMON! WAKE UP! Get on with it, boy."

"She isn't a scarecrow, and she isn't old," said Sally. "She's a good pony. She was my pony when I rode here . . ." but no one was paying any attention to her.

Miss Meek had tightened Clover's girth and Simon was mounting.

"We ride in the lane," Miss Meek said, and with her hand on Clover's bit ring began to walk towards the lane.

She knows Clover will try to bolt back to her box, Sally thought.

"Let him go," ordered Mr Knowles. "The boy can ride, you know."

"Keep an eye on her," Miss Meek warned Simon but she let go of the bit and walked in front of Clover.

The instant Miss Meek let go of her, Clover stopped dead.

Sally's nails bit into the palms of her hands. If she carts him back to the box Mr Knowles will never buy her, she thought.

Clover dropped her head, shied suddenly sideways, ready to spin round and bolt.

"Watch out!" yelled Thalia.

But in the instant, without appearing to do anything, no kicking, no yanking at his reins, Simon had Clover gathered together and trotting after Miss Meek.

Simon rode Clover up and down the lane in the same way. He seemed to do nothing but Clover changed from a walk to a trot, from a trot to a canter and back as if she were a dressage pony and Sally knew that Simon hadn't just been showing off when he had told her that he had won rosettes and cups. Simon really could ride.

"I've never seen Clover go so well for any child," Miss Meek said to Mr Knowles as they watched.

"Oh, he was a very good little rider," said Aunt Dot who had squeezed herself out of the back of the car to join them. "We were all so proud of him."

"Boy refuses to ride, that's the shame of it," said Mr Knowles. "Stubborn as a mule. Can't do a thing with him."

Simon rode back to the yard at an extended walk.

"Well?" demanded his father.

Sally held her breath waiting for Simon's reply, seeing Clover grazing in the paddock beside the Knowles's bungalow or being led back to her grazing strip while the Knowles's drove away.

Simon dismounted.

"I don't want a pony," he said, "but if you must buy me a pony I suppose it may as well be Clover."

"We'll take her on trial," said Mr Knowles. "The boy can ride her at the show on Saturday?"

Mr Knowles and Miss Meek arranged deposit and price.

"I'm so glad you're taking her," cried Sally. "She won't jump. You don't need to worry, I know she won't jump."

"I felt a lot better on her than I ever did on those tearaways that Dad was always hiring from Mr Frazer. Perhaps he'll leave me alone now. Perhaps it will satisfy him if I just ride around on Clover," and Simon smiled suddenly, giving Clover a fruit drop from his pocket and scratching under her mane. "You can be my pony and there won't be any more rows."

"I cannot imagine," said Thalia, being driven home in the back seat of Mr Lorimer's car, "how he could possibly have chosen Clover when his dad would have bought him any pony he wanted. Why doesn't he want a decent pony?"

"I told you about the accident," said Sally.

"Oh, I know! But to buy a pony like Clover!"

Sally didn't answer. She sat next to her father, her imagination filled with happiness. No longer would the thought of Clover left behind at Miss Meek's riding school haunt her dreams.

"And that's another day wasted when we should have been schooling," moaned Thalia. "We've hardly practised jumping as a pair. Hardly at all. And not tomorrow but the next day is the show!"

Chapter Seven

Next morning Sally and Thalia had brought in their ponies, fed them and left them with an armful of hay each while they went down to the field to build cross-country obstacles.

"Four will be enough," said Thalia, dragging out a broken branch from under the chestnut tree. "Make them broad so we can practise jumping together. That's what we've got to practise, jumping as a pair."

"You don't say," muttered Sally under her breath.

"Like Mrs Blair said, you've got to waken Willow up. It is a pairs competition we're riding in!"

Sally stopped piling up jumping poles into a solid mass.

"I do know," she stated, scowling at Thalia. "I heard Mrs Blair too. And I heard what she told you. You have to hold Tarquin back."

"Then where would we be? Not jumping anything! In a right mess! I have got to ride Tarquin on and you have got to keep Willow up with him. That is *if* you want to win. *If* we are trying to win the cup, you have got to keep up with me. Right?"

For a second Sally stared at Thalia, on the edge of telling her just what she thought of her bossiness but before she had gathered her words together Thalia was back in full voice.

"Brainwave," she shouted. "I've just thought. There's that old bench in the summerhouse. It would make a jump. Let's get it."

Ben, walking Meg and Misty, saw them struggling to carry the bench back to the field and came to help. In an hour they had created four reasonably solid jumps, all broad enough to be jumped as a pair.

After breakfast they rode down to the field. Sally was in a black mood. All through breakfast Thalia had gone on and on about how to ride a cross-country course and how vital it was to go round at a good gallop.

You'd think she was bloomin' Mrs Blair, Sally thought. Knowing everything. Always right. Boss, boss, bossing.

They schooled first, riding in circles at a walk and sitting trot. Sally's bad temper ran down her reins making Willow jib and shy at nothing. She walked with her head down, dragging her hooves and stumbling over tufts of grass.

"Oh, get on," Sally told her. "Willow, walk on," and she tugged at her reins, kicking Willow on, knowing that in a minute Thalia would be organising them into jumping. Never had Sally felt less like jumping. She knew she would be left behind, knew she would come off. Suddenly she wondered what Simon was doing, wondered if he would be schooling, or sitting in his bedroom worrying about tomorrow.

"Better if we each have a jump round first," stated Thalia. Tarquin flew over the obstacles more certain than a guided missile. Willow trotted and stopped; trotted and stopped, then on her third attempt she got in far too close to the jump and shot over it from a standstill, throwing Sally on to her neck and depositing her on to the ground on the other side of the jump.

"What a beginning," moaned Thalia in despair. "What's Mrs Blair going to think of us if you jump like that tomorrow?"

Remounting, Sally ignored her completely.

It was the middle of the afternoon when Mrs Lorimer and Jamie came to see how they were getting on. They were just in time to see Tarquin crash his way through the jumps while Willow trotting well behind him refused at the second and third jump and ran out at the fourth.

"That's useless," cried Thalia, not seeing Mrs Lorimer and Jamie. "How can we go to Tarent tomorrow and bug the whole thing up like that? It's you!"

"Are you meant to be a pair?" called Mrs Lorimer, taking in the bored, cross ponies, Thalia's temper and Sally's in-drawn silence.

"Yes we bloomin' well were. Huh, some pair," snorted Thalia not caring that it was Sally's mother she was speaking to.

"You don't think," said Mrs Lorimer, "that you've entered for the wrong class? Why on earth did you choose to enter a pairs class?"

"Seemed a good idea at the time," muttered Thalia.

"Can't you change your entry?"

"No way," snapped Thalia. "We've just got to go on trying to make them into a pair," and she swung Tarquin round, ready to jump again.

"I don't think so," said Mrs Lorimer in her most adult voice. "You've been jumping all day. No wonder they're fed up. Put them in their boxes and give them a rest."

"We've forgotten everything that Martine

86

taught us," said Sally as she led Willow back to the stables. "Not only me but you too."

"This is cross-country, not namby-pamby showjumping."

"We've to showjump too," exclaimed Sally, suddenly remembering.

"But it is the cross-country that really matters."

"Oh, I know, I know. Don't keep on going on!"

"Sorry," said Thalia not meaning it. "Sorry I spoke."

While they drank lemonade and ate Mrs Lorimer's cherry cake, Sally and Thalia didn't speak to each other. Thalia played noisily with the beardies. Sally stared out of the kitchen window to the long glimmering line of the sea.

In the early evening before they turned the ponies out they jumped over the battered obstacles for one last time. Although Sally did her best to keep Willow up with Tarquin he stormed ahead of her, his speed mocking Willow's neat, precise jumping.

"Better clean our tack," said Thalia

scornfully. "Then they won't be able to say it's as rubbish as our jumping."

As they stood in the tack room, dragging wet sponges down sweated reins, rubbing in the sharp-smelling saddle soap, polishing bits and stirrups, the silence between them settled into politeness.

"Please pass the saddle soap."

"Excuse me, could I have that sponge when you've finished with it?"

And even when Thalia upset the bucket of water Sally didn't giggle as she usually did, she just went on cleaning her saddle without looking round.

"Seven tomorrow morning?" said Thalia when all their tack was clean and the looseboxes brushed out.

"Yes," said Sally, wanting to stand and chat, wanting to talk about the show, about seeing Verity Blair again; about Simon and Clover. But Thalia was already marching away, her shoulders squared, her head held high.

"Are you two still quarrelling?" asked Mrs Lorimer as Sally came into the kitchen. "What's it all about?"

"Nothing," said Sally automatically.

"Seemed more than nothing to me," said her mother. "Simon's father is on the phone. Your dad's speaking to him."

Sally hurried into the hall. Sitting on the bottom step of the stairs she listened to her father saying, "Yes, of course. Yes. That would be no trouble at all. I'm sure the girls wouldn't mind in the least. Sally's here now. Do you want to speak to her? She knows more about the pony side of things than I do." Saying goodbye he handed the receiver to Sally.

"Hello," said Mr Knowles, his voice loud but not shouting. "We're having a bit of trouble here. Our trailer has cracked a wheel shaft so the boy will have to ride to the show. Want to fix it up that he meets you two. Make sure he gets there. Doesn't go skiving off."

"We're riding there," said Sally. "Of course we can meet him."

"There's a crossroads about two miles from the showground. Buxton's Free Range Eggs on one corner, Manor House Hotel on the other."

"Thalia will know."

"Right. That's fixed, then. Ten o'clock?"

"Yes," said Sally, hoping it would fit in with Thalia's timetable.

"Bye," said Mr Knowles.

"Clover?" demanded Sally. "How is Clover? Has she settled in? You are keeping her?"

"Depends what sort of performance they put up tomorrow. I've arranged for Simon to ride in the Handy Pony. Then we'll see about settling in or not. Here's Simon. Ask him."

"Yes," said Simon when Sally repeated her question. "She seems fine."

"We're going to meet you tomorrow."

"If I'm there," said Simon, and Sally couldn't tell whether his voice was frightened or joking.

"Of course you'll be there. You *must* ride in the Hand Pony or your father will send Clover back. Of course you're coming."

But Simon only said goodbye and put the phone down.

Sally's mother came to say goodnight.

She told her to hurry up and get into bed and not to worry about tomorrow.

For a long time Sally sat on the window seat staring out over the sea. Clouds gusting over the full moon made it race across the sky, made the sea shimmer and dusk and her crystal unicorn sparkle with moonlight.

The thought came to Sally that if she went down to the ponies' field Thalia would be there and they could make up. Pulling on her anorak Sally crept through the dark house and picked her way through pits of moon shadow, down to the field.

But there was no one there. Only Tarquin and Willow lying by the looped branches of the chestnut tree.

Sally leant on the field gate, swallowing back her disappointment, gazing at Tarquin's dark bulk and Willow's mothy whiteness.

This time tomorrow it would all be over. No matter what happened it would be over. But Sally didn't want it to be over, she wanted to be in the middle of it, in the middle of a day of winning and jumping, being with Thalia and Simon, a day to equal her imagination, a day that would go on and on for ever.

"If it's anything like today," Sally thought as she turned to walk slowly back to Kestrels, "it will be a disaster. Total, absolute disaster."

Chapter Eight

Sally's stomach was churning when she woke. Today was Tarent Show. Today she was going to showjump and ride cross-country. And last night she had quarrelled with Thalia. She lay flat on her back staring up at the white ceiling. It was Thalia's fault as much as her own, Tarquin's as much as Willow's. Thalia would need to hold him back, steady him, if they were ever going to jump as a pair.

Then Sally remembered Simon – that he was riding Clover in the Handy Pony, that he had to do well or his father would send Clover back to Miss Meek's; that they had to meet him.

If he comes at all, Sally thought, jumping out of bed. But he must, he must do well, Clover must never go back to Miss Meek's.

By the time Sally reached the stables Thalia had brought in both ponies.

"Narg says I've to apologise for going on at you."

"Mum said the same thing. We've to stop being so stupid."

"Right," said Thalia. "Forget it. OK?"

"Forgotten," said Sally.

"Absolutely," said Thalia. But it wasn't.

"Mr Knowles phoned Dad last night," said Sally, the words rushing out of her to fill up the bad-tempered space that was still between them. "Their trailer has broken down, so we've to meet Simon at crossroads at ten o'clock by a free range egg farm and a hotel. I said you'd know where it was."

"Oh, no!" groaned Thalia. "Why didn't you say we'd see him at the show? It's always such a faff meeting someone like that. If they're not there you never know what's happened to them."

"I would think," said Sally before she could stop herself, "when someone had saved your pony from being sucked down into a swamp you wouldn't care how long you had to wait for him."

"Spoils it all," sulked Thalia. "Suppose we meet Verity. She won't want to hang about waiting and Tarquin will be fed up if we have to wait. It'll put him in a bad mood for the day."

Any minute now, thought Sally irritably, she'll be telling me to keep up with her in the pairs, and she left Thalia grumbling to herself while she started work on Willow's mane and tail.

By half-past nine they were riding down the tree-shaded drive from Kestrels to the main road. Their ponies were groomed to perfection, manes and tails catching the breeze like silken strands; coats gleaming; their polished tack shining and their hoofs oiled. Mr and Mrs Lorimer with Ben, Em and Jamie were coming to the show bringing a picnic but only staying until around two because Em had to be taken to a party. Thalia's narg was going to a motorbike rally so would not be there at all.

Tarquin walked out with long, reaching strides, Thalia's heels niggling his sides to keep him in front of Willow. When they reached the road Thalia let Tarquin trot on, his hoofs ringing on the metalled road. Willow battered behind him, tossing her head, almost cantering to keep up with him.

"Here! Wait for us!" Sally shouted. "Willow's nearly sweating."

Thalia steaded Tarquin to a jog trot.

"The showjumping starts at eleven and our class is first. If we don't keep going we'll be late," she called back over her shoulder.

"They'll be worn out if you keep on at this rate," Sally muttered but Thalia paid no attention to her.

They had been riding for almost half an hour when Tarquin went lame. Sally noticed it first hearing the difference in his hoof beats.

"Rubbish," snapped Thalia. "Tarquin's never lame."

But he was and in a few minutes Thalia had to admit it. She stopped Tarquin and jumped to the ground.

"Near fore," said Sally sliding down from Willow.

Thalia glared at Sally but this time she didn't argue. She picked up Tarquin's foot and there was a chipping stone wedged between his shoe and the sole of his foot.

"Hoof pick, nurse," said Thalia, being a television doctor, but Sally did not have a hoof pick and although they tried knocking the chipping with a bigger stone from the side of the verge and working on it with a branch it remained firmly wedged under the rim of Tarquin's shoe.

A car passed and Thalia waved her arms wildly, shouting for help but it sped past ignoring them.

"Putrid parsnips," Thalia yelled after it. "Punctures in all your tyres!"

Four more cars drove past before a rusty, tea-cosy car shuddered to a halt. A square woman in a tweed hat got out and asked what was wrong.

"It's a stone," explained Thalia. "Stuck in his shoe and we can't get it out."

"What you need is a boy scout," said the square woman braying with laughter at her own wit.

"We're on our way to Tarent Show," said Thalia urgently. "I'm going to be late for the showjumping. You must have something in your car that would hook it out."

"Something in your picnic basket," suggested Sally seeing a wicker basket on the back seat.

"Tin opener!" exclaimed the woman and in seconds she had rustled out a solid, old-fashioned tin opener and while Thalia held up Tarquin's foot she levered out the stone.

The chipping came out so suddenly that the square woman staggered backwards almost sitting down on the road.

Sally grabbed her arm to steady her but Thalia had already mounted and was trotting away shouting her thanks.

"Couldn't wait," she cried when Sally caught up with her. "It's twenty past ten. We're never going to be in time for the jumping. It'll be over before we get there," and she urged Tarquin into a canter.

Willow trotting like a hackney pony battered along behind him.

"You're going too fast. You shouldn't be cantering on the road," but Thalia didn't choose to hear.

The board advertising Buxton's Free Range Eggs was painted red and white, not to be missed. It was definitely where they were to meet Simon but there was no sign of him.

"Told you," shouted Thalia pulling Tarquin to a jagged halt. "It's always a mess trying to meet someone. We're so late I expect he's got fed up waiting for us and gone on."

"He wouldn't do that," said Sally, looking around anxiously for any sign of Simon.

Sally felt everything was wrong – her stirrups uneven, her hard hat digging into the back of her neck, her stomach clenched into a solid, nervous lump – and it was all Thalia's fault for riding like an idiot.

"Well, he's not here, is he? Come on. We can't wait," and as she spoke Thalia was riding Tarquin towards the road signposted for the show.

"But I said we would wait."

"Not when we're so late! Oh, come on. Simon doesn't need us. Come on." Willow pawed the road, whinnying and fretting to follow Tarquin. For a moment Sally was tempted, then she remembered Clover.

"We must wait," she shouted. "If we're not here Simon won't go to the show and they'll send Clover back to Miss Meek's."

"Well, I'm not waiting," and Thalia eased her reins letting Tarquin plunge forward.

Once the sound of Tarquin's hoofs had faded into silence Willow stopped messing about and stood still, clinking her bit impatiently.

"Only a minute," Sally promised, clapping Willow's sweated shoulder.

"Only a minute and he'll be here. Pretty rotten of Thalia. How would she like it if Simon had promised to meet her and then just ridden on?"

One minute turned into five minutes. Five minutes into ten. Horses and riders trotted past Sally, all smart and bright, all bound for the show. People looked down curiously from horsebox windows at Sally standing on the grass verge holding Willow's reins.

At last Sally remounted.

"No use," she said to Willow. "He's not coming."

Then clear in her mind's eye she saw Clover standing in her narrow stall at the riding school, her tail matted, her eyes dead as she waited for another stranger to ride her up and down the lane. Sally shuddered, goose over her grave.

"No!" she said aloud. "No!"

A young woman on a bay hunter pointed out which road would take her in the direction of the Moss. Sally urged Willow into a trot and rode away from the crossroads. She was going to find

Simon. She was going to make him come to the show.

The road turned sharply to the left over a hump-backed bridge and there, sitting in a field gateway, was Simon holding Clover's reins as she cropped the grass.

"Simon!" yelled Sally. "What's wrong? Why are you here? You were meant to meet us at the crossroads. We're late. Really late. Come on."

Simon looked straight at Sally and she saw his face was white and strained, his eyes pink-rimmed.

"I'm not going to the show," he said. "I'm not riding."

Fervently Sally wished that Thalia was with her. She would have raged at Simon and made him ride. But there was only herself. Sally took a deep breath.

"Don't you care?" she demanded turning on Simon. "Don't you care about Clover? If you don't come to the show your dad will send Clover back. Maybe it was your fault that your pony broke its leg. I don't know. But it *will* be your fault if Clover is sent back to the riding school. All you have to do is ride round the Handy Pony and you've saved her. If you won't do that you'll know it is your fault this time. Your fault if Clover is sent back. And when they've worked and worked for Miss Meek she sends them to the sales and you know what that means."

Simon sat without moving.

"Now. Come on, now!" ordered Sally.

Suddenly she remembered the unicorn lying secret in her jacket pocket. She scrabbled it out and it lay in her hand, its green jewelled eye glinting up at her. She leant down to Simon.

"Hold out your hand," she told Simon, and placed the unicorn on his palm. "It came out of the sea. You can keep it for today. It makes your wishes come true."

For a long minute Simon stared down at the brilliant, rainbowed unicorn, then he closed his hand over it.

"Right," Simon said looking up at Sally. "OK."

He thrust the unicorn into his pocket and sprang to his feet.

"I'm doing this for you," he muttered to Clover, his hands shaking as he pulled up his girths. "Wouldn't much care to be sent back to that riding school myself."

Twenty minutes later Tarent Show lay spread out in front of them. It was far bigger than Sally had ever imagined – billowing white tents, patchwork of show rings, every size and shape of horse and pony and a menagerie of beasts from haystack Highland cattle to varnished pigs.

No one paid any attention to them as they rode through the open gates and on past rows of stalls until they reached the juvenile showjumping ring. A dark-skinned boy on a flashy chestnut was jumping in the ring.

As Sally steadied Willow to a halt she felt her throat tighten, her mouth go suddenly dry. Worrying about Clover she had almost forgotten that she was here to jump. That she had never really jumped in public before. The red and white poles grew before her eyes into enormous White City jumps, stretching skywards, filling the ring in strange patterns of doubles and trebles.

Never, never could she jump those, Sally decided. They must be for a different class. They were far too high for Willow.

The boy rode out of the ring. A loud speaker crackled and a voice announced, "Last call for Sally Lorimer. Sally Lorimer number 69 to ring 4."

Chapter Nine

The announcement broke over Sally like an icy wave.

"But I'm not ready," she said aloud. "Willow's not ready. We've only just got here," and she stood up in her stirrups searching for Thalia, thinking that Thalia could go and tell them that she wasn't jumping.

"There you are at last!" Mrs Blair came striding towards her. "Where have you been? Never mind. Tell me later. Thalia saw to your entry and I've got your number."

"I'm not . . ." began Sally but Mrs Blair was already tying number 69 round her arm.

"Nice little course. Jumps are numbered. Round the outside, then across the centre over the double, back down over the wall and that's it. Let's have another clear round for the jump-off."

"But Willow's never . . ."

"On you go dear," said Mrs Blair. She gripped Willow's bit-ring and marched them to the entrance, then with a clap on Willow's quarters she sent them trotting into the ring.

For a second Sally had only one thought in her head, to get off Willow. Once she was on the ground no one could make her jump.

"That's what you did before," said the voice in Sally's head. "You're not going to mess things up like that again, are you?"

And Sally knew she couldn't. She was here and she had to jump.

A steward blew a whistle and somehow Willow had carried her through the start and with pricked ears, bright eyes, Willow was cantering at the first jump.

Sally's reins were too long, fistfuls of leather that she couldn't sort out. Her feet were loose in her stirrups and as Willow jumped Sally collapsed on her neck. There was the crash of falling poles behind them and Willow was racing on to the next jump.

As they turned up the far side of the ring Sally was completely out of control. She hardly knew where she was. The red and white poles seemed to rush at her and as Willow jumped Sally hung on to her mane, waiting for the crash of poles falling behind them and the gasping, indrawn breath of the spectators.

At the top of the ring Sally hardly knew what to do next. She could only hear Mrs Blair's voice filling her head, telling her that she had to cross the ring jumping the double. She hauled Willow round but at the first part of the double Willow swerved to one side and galloped past the jump.

Voices were shouting at Sally to stop. Someone was blowing a whistle. Sally caught a glimpse of Thalia's shocked face, Verity Blair standing beside her.

Only the wall. I've got to jump it and then I've been round, Sally told herself. She tugged madly on one rein and turned Willow straight at the wall. In two bucking, galloping strides Willow was right under the wall. She rose straight into the air. For a second Sally seemed to hang in space – clear of the saddle, hands under her chin, clutching the buckle of her reins, one stirrup flying loose and her scream frozen in her throat. Clear over the wall Sally crashed down on to the saddle and was carried out of the ring.

"Number 69, Sally Lorimer, is eliminated for taking the wrong course."

Sally tumbled to the ground, threw her arms round Willow's neck and pressed her face against her mane. It was only now that Sally realised that she had been crying. It had all been too sudden. She hadn't been ready, hadn't had time. The sound of crashing poles was still loud in her ears; her eyes still blurred by the brightness of the enormous jumps.

"Ladies and gentlemen, now that we have rebuilt the course we have the jump-off for first place. Number 68, Thalia Nisbet and number 53, Verity Blair."

Sally blew her nose, scrubbed at her eyes and looking straight ahead so that no one could see her, she found a place by the ringside just in time to see Thalia win the toss and Verity ride in.

Buster cleared all the jumps from a solid canter but he had two refusals. Tarquin pranced into the ring, mane and tail flying as he struggled against Thalia's control, then with a half-rear he was away, following an arching rainbow-path round the whole course. Thalia's face was swallowed up in an excited grin.

"Clear round number 68, Thalia Nisbet on Tarquin, our winner and, I should think our fastest round."

People clapped, rosettes were presented and a short burst of marching music crashed out over the loudspeaker.

Jealous? Sally asked herself.

No, she answered honestly. Just wish I hadn't made such a muck-up; hadn't let Willow down.

But you waited for Simon, consoled the voice. Because you waited for him it'll be OK for Clover. They'll keep her.

"Hi!" yelled Thalia riding up with Verity, her whole being radiant with success.

"You were super. Tarquin just flew over them," said Sally, truly meaning it.

"Your pony jumped well," said Verity to Sally, "She jumped miles over the wall."

"We've to give our names in at the Light Horse tent," said Thalia, not mentioning Sally's performance. "Be back in a minute."

Sally stood watching them ride away together. Verity should be Thalia's partner for the cross-country, she thought. Be better than me.

Sally looked at her watch. It was nearly twelve. The pairs cross-country started at two. Two hours and she would be riding with Thalia over walls and barrels, drop jumps and banks. Sally shuddered and wrapped her arms tightly round herself as she watched other children riding up to Sally and Verity to congratulate them.

She didn't want to wait for Thalia. Sally mounted Willow, turned her in the opposite direction and began to ride slowly through the crowded life of the show. She leant down over Willow's neck and fed her a peppermint.

"It was all my fault," she whispered. "You were the best pony."

Vaguely Sally was looking for the Handy Pony class. She hadn't seen Simon since they had ridden into the show. By now he would have ridden round the Handy Pony and Clover would be safe.

If he hasn't bolted, she thought.

"Sal! Sally!" called Emma running through the crowd towards Sally. "We've been looking for you for ages. We've got the picnic. Come on. Thalia's looking for you too. Buck up. We can't stay long because of my party."

Sally rode beside her sister to where her family were sitting on the grass around a rug spread out on the ground covered with picnic food. Her mother was filling rolls with home-made spreads and lettuce. Ben was holding Meg and Misty.

Sally swallowed hard to clear the lump in her throat before she began to tell them about her disastrous round. But they knew already.

"Bad luck," said her father. "Thalia and Thalia's red rosette told us."

"Least you didn't fall off," said Ben.

Sally wanted to say, Wait for the cross-country, but her voice wasn't there. She looked away dragging her hand across her eyes.

"Been looking for you everywhere," cried Thalia, pulling Tarquin to a halt just in time to stop him plunging through the picnic. "We've to have lunch with the Blairs. All the Pony Club lot are there. They want you to come so they can get to know us."

Sally shook her head.

"Why not?" demanded Thalia impatiently. "It's good. They all like Willow."

"No."

"Stick then," said Thalia and galloped off.

"Is there a rift in the lute?" asked Mr Lorimer and his wife gave him a quick look, warning him not to cause trouble.

Sitting close to Meg, Sally shared her food between dogs and pony. In spite of the sun she was cold. Cold and afraid. Afraid of the cross-country. If things went wrong as they had that morning Willow could easily fall and break a leg.

"Are you sure you're feeling all right?" asked her mother. "If you're not feeling well I'm sure we could find some way of getting Willow home to Kestrels and you could come with us in the car."

"Of course not," said Sally. "I'm fine."

"Well," said her father standing up. "We'll need to go if we're going to get Em to this party on time. Now, do be sensible. You don't have to ride in this cross-country thing if you don't feel like it."

"I'm fine," Sally repeated.

She watched them pack the picnic and go back to the car.

"Fine," she told herself again when her family had gone, "Fine, fine, fine. I'm Thalia's pair and I must ride round with her."

But Sally's head was filled with the sound of crashing poles. This afternoon the obstacles would be solid. They wouldn't knock down.

Chapter Ten

"Don't tell me you're not ready! The Junior Cross-country's nearly finished and then it's the pairs." Thalia's hard hat was under her arm and her hair blazed round her head as she sat tall in the saddle. "We've still got to ride them in."

Sally stared up at the silhouette of Thalia and Tarquin looming over her.

Just tell her that you're not riding. Say you're not feeling well. Tell her your father is coming back for you . . . whispered the tempter in Sally's head.

She opened her mouth ready to make excuses to Thalia; to say anything,

anything as long as she didn't have to ride over the cross-country.

Do not be such a coward, said a voice that was deeper than Sally's mind, deeper than herself. Willow will take you round. Give in now and you'll hate yourself for ever. Remember what it was like when you wouldn't gallop? Well?

"Glory gosh," exclaimed Sally struggling to her feet. "I didn't know it was that time." She mounted quickly and, gathering in her reins, clapped Willow's shoulder.

"Right," she said to Thalia, "where shall we go?"

"Bit of space over here," said Thalia leading the way. "Why didn't you come and have lunch with us?"

Bumping behind Tarquin Sally hardly heard a word Thalia was saying. She had forgotten everything she had ever known about riding, absolutely everything Martine had taught her.

Over to her left Sally could see the cross-country course laid out over the hillside – brush jumps, barrels, ditches, walls and the sheen of a water jump. No one was jumping. Stewards were going round altering the obstacles. Sally supposed the junior class was over and they were getting the course ready for the pairs.

If only I wasn't a pair, Sally thought desperately as she trotted and cantered Willow in a schooling circle. Then it wouldn't matter. Thalia could jump and it wouldn't matter what I did.

"Junior Pairs Cross-country," boomed the loudspeaker. "To the cross-country course now. This is class 15. About to commence – class 15."

"That's us," said Thalia. "May as well go now," and Willow followed Tarquin towards the start.

"What did you think of the stile?" Thalia called back over her shoulder. "They've never seen a stile before and it's more or less straight into the water when they land."

"Stile?" echoed Sally, not knowing what Thalia was talking about.

Thalia looked back at Sally's blank face.

"Don't tell me that you haven't walked the course?" she exclaimed, her voice light and false. "I was sure you'd have walked round with Em or Ben."

It took Sally a minute to take in what Thalia had done – walked round the course without coming to tell her; walked round with the Blairs!

"Of all the stinking, disgusting things . . ." Sally began, then bit back her words. Nothing she could say could possibly be bad enough. She glared furiously at Thalia.

"You know," she said, spitting out the words, "you know that I haven't seen the jumps; that I would never have thought of walking round the course. What a rotten thing to do. Just so you could be with the Blairs."

Through the throngs of ponies, parents and children gathered round the start, Sally caught sight of Simon trotting Clover towards them. In her fear of the cross-country Sally had completely forgotten about him. There was a blue rosette on Clover's bridle and Simon was beaming with success.

"You did it," cried Sally. "Oh, good! Good for Clover. Your father will have to keep her now."

"And I jumped. Fidgy two inch pole but I jumped it!"

"We've to go next," said Thalia. "I'll just have to tell you what jumps are next."

"Wait!" and Simon took the unicorn out of his pocket and gave it back to Sally. "Pure brill. Magic," he said.

For a second Sally looked at it, rainbow in the palm of her hand, its golden horn glinting. She slipped it back into her pocket and rode Willow to the start.

Thalia held Tarquin on a tight rein. He was all energy, desperate to gallop and jump. Willow, too, pranced and pawed the ground, sensing Tarquin's excitement. Willow's ears were pricked and her eyes bright as she gazed out over the course, every bit as keen to gallop and to jump as Tarquin.

"I'll count to three and then blow my whistle," said a wrinkled woman with straight, white hair pulled back into a long ponytail.

Sally was still too furious even to look at Thalia. Her mind was filled with thoughts of Thalia's bossiness and nagging.

"Keep Willow up . . ." muttered Thalia.

"Don't you tell me what to do! Don't you bloomin' dare. You wouldn't even wait for Simon. You went off with the Blairs . . ."

The whistle cut through Sally's fury and instantly she had ridden Willow forward, plunging at Tarquin's side, urging Willow on.

The first jump, a stone wall, raced at Sally. Nerves flickered in her stomach but she was too mad with Thalia to notice.

Both ponies soared over the wall taking it in their stride like steeplechasers. They landed neck and neck. Sally never moved in the saddle. She jumped the wall as Thalia jumped, almost a part of her pony.

The course swung to the right. Rustic poles were in front of them and then behind.

"Brush next," shouted Thalia but

almost before she had spoken Sally felt Willow rise and reach out over the brush fence.

If the showjumping had been a blurred maze of jumps the cross-country lay before Sally like a magic way, an enchanted path. Their galloping ponies were winged to carry them high and clear over every obstacle.

"Next one's a drop," yelled Thalia. "Then downhill."

Sally glanced across at her, laughing for the joy and speed of their galloping and Thalia was grinning, laughing, caught in the same shared speed, this brilliant delight.

Willow leapt out over the drop and Sally felt the world fall away from her. They seemed to hang suspended in air before Willow's hoofs touched the ground again and they bucketed on downhill.

There was a jump of upended barrels and then a low turf bank which both ponies jumped – reaching heads, tucked-up knees – exactly side by side.

As they came to the stile Tarquin's

gallop slowed to a canter, his eyes goggled and he snorted suspiciously through wide nostrils.

Out of the corner of her eye Sally saw him slowing down, his front legs propping as he tried to swing to the side, but Thalia's legs, seat and voice drove him on.

Suddenly Sally realised that she was in front. It was up to her to get Willow over the stile and then Tarquin would follow.

"On you go," she whispered, sitting hard and neat in the saddle, riding her willing pony straight at the stile.

With a flick of her ears and swish of her tail Willow was over and as Sally trotted on into the wide stretch of water she heard Tarquin land and come storming up behind her showering her with spray.

Never again could Thalia taunt Sally for being too slow. It was Willow who had given Tarquin a lead. Willow who had shown Tarquin the way.

They both cleared the in and out mini sheep pen, then leaping back over the first wall at a different place they galloped through the finish together.

They slid from their ponies laughing and gasping.

"We were brill!" exclaimed Thalia. "I knew we could do it. I kept telling you all you had to do was to keep up with Tarquin."

"And give him a lead!"

"He didn't stop. I kept him going. It wasn't a refusal."

"Clear Round," triumphed Sally.

"I reckon," said Thalia.

They stood for a moment grinning at each other, not speaking.

"Listen," said Thalia, the words bursting out of her. "I didn't mean to be so rotten to you. Going on and on about Willow being slow. Honestly I didn't mean to say some of the things I did. I just get all worked up and say things I don't mean afterwards. I get so desperate for Tarquin to do well. It's a way of saying thank you to Narg for being bothered with me. And I knew that if you would only wake Willow—" Thalia clapped her hand over her mouth.

"I shan't say anything, ever again,"

Thalia mumbled through her fingers. "I shall buy a gag for myself and wear it always."

"That," said Sally, "would make you the most boring friend and Tarquin would hate it if you couldn't talk to him! Anyway you were right, even if you did go on a bit."

And in the excitement of the moment their days of quarrelling were forgotten. For now Sally was as good a rider as Thalia; Willow as fast as Tarquin.

Simon's father came to shout his thanks to Sally for finding Clover.

"Boy's keen again!" he roared. "Miracle! Miracle!"

"You will keep Clover?"

"Home with us until the day she dies. Give you my word."

Verity came to tell them that they were the fastest pair and at last, when all the scores were in, they knew they had won. The only clear round out of eighteen entries.

The woman with the white ponytail presented their rosettes and a silver cup to be shared six months each. Mrs Blair shook their hands, told them her heart had been in her mouth watching them going round and Sally pinched herself hard to make sure she wasn't dreaming.

"Now," said Mrs Blair looking at Thalia, "come over to my box. I want to have a word with you about our Pony Club team for the one day event in November. I'm wondering if this year we might, just might . . ."

Thalia urged Tarquin forward at Mrs Blair's side. Three fat women on Highland ponies, giggling together, rode in front of Sally and by the time they had ridden past, Thalia and Mrs Blair were lost in the crowd. Sally, clutching the cup, was alone.

It's because I made such a mess of the jumping this morning, Sally thought. It's because they know I'm nervous.

She clenched her teeth and swallowed hard.

Don't care, she thought. I don't care if they don't want me.

She shivered, suddenly cold. No longer

part of the bright day; no longer part of the milling life of the show.

"Sally!" Thalia pulled Tarquin to a rearing halt beside her. "What are you doing here? Didn't you hear Mrs Blair?"

"That was you, not me."

"Oh, idiot nit! She wants you too," and Thalia stared at Sally, seeing her hurt disappointment. "I've told you I'm sorry for the things I said. And I am. Honest I am. I couldn't wait for Simon. It wasn't because I didn't care about him. I just had to get to the showjumping in time. I don't know why I walked round the course with the Blairs. I was coming to get you, honest. Then they shouted that there wasn't time and ... And I'm sorry you had to give Tarquin a lead over the stile because that makes Willow a better pony than him."

"Well, equal," said Sally grinning.

"Willow more equal," said Thalia.

And they were both laughing.

"OK?" said Thalia, and this time it was.

They rode home together, taking it in turns to carry the cup, Sally's red rosette safe in her pocket beside the unicorn.

When they had seen to their ponies they left them chomping pony-nuts, oats and bran.

"Dear Willow," murmured Sally turning back for one last loving look at her pony – the flat cheekbone, the arch of her neck, the curve of her ears. "Thank you for everything." She swung away to chase after Thalia and run with her to Kestrels.

They burst into the house together.

"We won the pairs!" shouted Thalia. "We were the best!"

"And Mrs Blair wants us to be in the Pony Club team," cried Sally to her astonished family. "Both of us!"

Together Sally and Thalia raced through Kestrels, Meg and Misty barking at their heels, Jamie running behind them as they stamped their way up the wide staircase.

"Pony Club Team! Pony Club Team!" they chanted. "Pony Club Team!"